"A superbly told story . . ."

100 Best Books, Young Book Trust

'Larger-than-life characters leap from the pages of this engaging and humorous story"   *Junior Education*

'Dick King-Smith at his best: an ingenious account of the way rabbits got to Australia. Don't be deceived by its apparent simplicity: it stands reading and re-reading, and each time you chuckle at something different"

Independent Weekend

'Sparkling humour and wonderful characters are Dick King-Smith's trademarks"   *Books for Your Children*

'Dick King-Smith has brought magic into the lives of millions of children"   *Parents Magazine*

'Here is an author who has earned his stripes in the world of animal writing, so you know you'll be in for a good read"   *Belfast Telegraph*

***All Because of Jackson* won the Bronze Medal for the 6–8 age category of the 1996 Smarties Book Prize.**

www.kidsatrandomhouse.co.uk

D0228276

Also available by Dick King-Smith,
award-winning author and creator of *Babe*:

From Corgi Pups, for beginner readers
Happy Mouseday

From Young Corgi/Doubleday Books
The Adventurous Snail
Billy the Bird
The Catlady
Connie and Rollo
E.S.P.
Funny Frank
The Guard Dog
Hairy Hezekiah
Horse Pie
Omnibombulator
Titus Rules OK

From Corgi Yearling Books
Mr Ape
A Mouse Called Wolf
Harriet's Hare

From Corgi Books, for older readers
Godhanger
The Crowstarver

Dick King-Smith

All Because
of Jackson

Illustrated by John Eastwood

ALL BECAUSE OF JACKSON
A YOUNG CORGI BOOK 978 0 552 55429 9

First published in Great Britain by Doubleday,
an imprint of Random House Children's Books

Doubleday edition published 1995
Young Corgi edition published 1997

This edition published 2006

5 7 9 10 8 6

Mixed Sources
Product group from well-managed
forests and other controlled sources
www.fsc.org Cert no. TT-COC-2139
© 1996 Forest Stewardship Council
FSC

The Random House Group Limited makes every effort to ensure that the papers
used in its books are made from trees that have been legally sourced from
well-managed and credibly certified forests. Our paper procurement policy
can be found at: www.randomhouse.co.uk/paper.htm

Set in 15/20pt Palatino by
Falcon Oast Graphic Art Ltd.

Young Corgi Books are published by Random House Children's Books,
61-63 Uxbridge Road, London W5 5SA

a division of The Random House Group Ltd

Addresses for companies within The Random House Group Limited
can be found at: www.randomhouse.co.uk

THE RANDOM HOUSE GROUP Limited Reg. No. 954009
www.kidsatrandomhouse.co.uk

A CIP catalogue record for this book is available from the British Library.

Printed and bound in the UK by CPI Mackays, Chatham ME5 8TD

CHAPTER ONE

Jackson was a seaside rabbit.

He was born in a sandy burrow on top of a cliff, and as soon as he was old enough to come out and sit on the grass and look down at the sea, he was fascinated by it.

While his brothers and sisters played about in the clifftop field, Jackson would sit by himself and watch the waves rolling in to break upon the sandy shore.

He watched the tides go in and out, he watched the seabirds wheeling and diving, and especially he watched the tall sailing-ships gliding past in the distance. How beautiful they are, thought Jackson. How I should love to run away to sea and be a sailor.

He consulted his mother.

"Mama," he said.

"Yes, Jackson?"

"There are men on those ships, aren't there?"

"Yes, Jackson. Sailors."

"I should like to be a sailor, Mama."

"Silly boy," said Jackson's mother. "Rabbits don't go on ships."

"But, Mama, the sea is in my blood."

"You go on a ship," said his mother, "and your blood will be in the sea. Men eat rabbits."

Jackson went away to think about this. I could hide, he thought. There must be lots of places to hide in a big sailing-ship. I could be a stowaway. I won't tell Mama or Papa. I'll just go.

So he did.

He set off across the clifftop field very early one morning, determined to find where the sailing-ships came in. That evening, climbing wearily to the top of a far headland, he looked down and saw before him just what he wanted.

There below was a wide bay, and on its shores a large seaside town with a great

harbour, in which lay a number of tall ships.

Tired out, Jackson found an empty rabbit burrow and crawled into it.

"Tomorrow," he murmured as he drifted into sleep, "tomorrow I shall go aboard my ship."

CHAPTER TWO

That night Jackson had the weirdest dream.

He was, it seemed, in a strange country, not cool and rainy like his homeland, but dry and very hot. Suddenly he saw the most extraordinary animal.

It was as tall as a man, with reddish fur, ears like a donkey, and a face like a sheep. Its arms were short, and it stood upright, balanced upon two enormously strong legs and a long, thick tail. Then the dream turned into a nightmare, for the monstrous creature began to come towards him, not walking, nor running, but hopping in huge bounds on those great hind legs. And as it drew near, Jackson could see something even more frightening. On the animal's stomach was a sort of pocket, and out of this pocket poked another head, with ears like a baby donkey and a face like a lamb!

Jackson woke with a squeal of terror.

"What's eating you?" said a voice, and there beside him in the burrow was

another rabbit, a young doe of about his own age.

"I was having a bad dream," he said.

"In my burrow," said the other.

"Oh, sorry!" said Jackson. "I didn't know. By the way, my name's Jackson."
"Funny sort of name."

"Not really. My father's called Jack. Anyway, who are you?"

"My mother doesn't believe in naming

children," said the young doe. "She's had so many, she can't be bothered. She just calls us all 'Bunny'."

"Bunny?" said Jackson. "That's nice. I like it." And I like you, he thought. I wonder if . . .

"You don't fancy going to sea, do you, Bunny?" he said.

"To sea?"

"In a ship. To sail away over the ocean."

"Where to?" said Bunny.

"I don't know," replied Jackson. "That'll be half the fun of it, not knowing."

"But rabbits don't go on ships," said Bunny.

"This one's going to," said Jackson.

"I want to sail the seas. I want to see the world."

"You're crazy," Bunny said. But nice, she thought.

"Well," she said, "it'll be daylight before very long. We'd better get started."

When they reached the town, Jackson and Bunny hopped through the empty silent streets until, as dawn was breaking, they reached the docks.

"Look!" cried Jackson as they made their way along the cobbled quay. "There's a ship!"

Tied up alongside was a great three-masted sailing-ship, whose sides towered above the two little rabbits.

"How ever shall we get aboard?" said Bunny.

"The same way that the sailors do," said Jackson. "Follow me!" And he ran along the quay until he reached the foot of a long, narrow, wooden gangplank. It was nearly broad daylight by now and there were noises on board, bangings and knockings and men's voices and footsteps.

"Quick!" said Jackson. "Up we go!" And up they went, scampering up the gangplank on whose side was fixed a large printed notice.

Brave British Hearts!
To all those of an
Adventurous Spirit
wishing to seek their fortunes and start a new life in a fur country, take note that the Peninsular & Oriental Navigation Company's Clipper
Atalanta
will set sail for
AUSTRALIA
on the
Third day of April 1842

The moment that Jackson and Bunny reached the top of the gangplank, they saw to their horror a number of sailors busy swabbing down the decks. Luckily the men's backs were towards the two rabbits, who instantly dashed for cover.

A frightened rabbit goes straight underground, and though here there was no

ground to go under, Jackson saw nearby a large, square, black hole, and into it he dived head first, Bunny following. Down the hatch they fell.

As well as passengers, the *Atalanta* was carrying in her hold goods for the settlers in Australia, and, luckily for the rabbits (for they fell a long way), it was a

cargo of bales of cloth. On these Jackson and Bunny landed and bounced.

"Are you all right, Bunny?" gasped Jackson.

"Yes, I think so. Where are we?"

"In a very big burrow by the look of things," said Jackson. "A good place for us to stow away, I should think."

"Would you?" said Bunny.

"Well, yes. We can hide amongst all this

stuff. No-one will ever find us. We can spend the whole voyage down here."

"And at the end of the voyage," said Bunny, "how exactly do we get out again?"

Jackson looked up at the open hatch, high above. He scratched one ear thoughtfully with a hind foot.

"Ah," he said.

"And while we're down here," went on Bunny, "what exactly do we eat?"

"Ah," said Jackson again.

"Or drink?"

"Ah," said Jackson. "Yes. Hm." But before he could add to this, they heard the sound of footsteps on the deck above, and voices, and then suddenly the square of daylight vanished as the hatch cover was put back, leaving the hold of the ship in darkness.

"It had better be a very short voyage," said Bunny. "Otherwise it would seem to me that, without food or water, we shall not see much of the world after all. We shall simply die down here. And all because of you, Jackson."

CHAPTER FOUR

All that morning the two rabbits hopped about in the gloom, exploring the great stack of bales of cloth that covered the floor of the hold, and finding nothing else.

Above them, there was much hustle and bustle on deck as the passengers came aboard, and then, around midday, a sudden great crash of sound as a brass band struck up on the quayside.

In amongst its noise the rabbits could hear voices bellowing orders, and the cries of farewell of those who were leaving and of those who had come to wave them goodbye.

Then, when the music had stopped and the shouts and calls had died away, peace and quiet returned as the *Atalanta* nosed her way out of harbour, and set sail for her journey to the opposite side of the world.

Down in the hold, Jackson and Bunny felt the motion as the clipper met the open sea, and heard the creaking of her timbers. Squatting side by side on a bale of cloth, the rabbits rose and fell as the ship swooped and dipped over the waves.

"Jackson," said Bunny.

"Yes?"

"I don't feel very well."

"Me neither."

"I don't think I'm a very good sailor."

"Nor me."

"I wish I hadn't come."

"Me too," said Jackson. "I'm sorry I got you into all this, Bunny. It's all my fault. I shall regret it for the rest of my life."

Bunny snuggled up to him.

"Don't worry," she said. "That won't be long."

By the following day the rabbits had grown used to the motion of the ship. They had also grown extremely hungry and thirsty.

When the ship had been some days at sea, the captain ordered an inspection of the various holds, to see that each was watertight and that their cargo had not shifted.

By now too weak and miserable to care, the rabbits watched helplessly as the hatch cover was removed, and a seaman climbed down a ladder, carrying a lantern.

A big, bearded man, he shone the light about as he examined the bales of cloth, and then its beam fell full upon the wretched stowaways.

"Well, I never!" said the seaman softly. "You'll make a nice meal, my hearties, you will!"

CHAPTER FIVE

Afterwards, Jackson and Bunny couldn't really remember what happened, so weak and helpless were they.

In fact, the bearded seaman found a sack and popped them in it, and climbed the ladder out of the hold, only to meet the first mate at the hatchway.

"All shipshape down below, Jenkins?" said the mate.

"Aye, aye, sir," replied Jenkins.

"What have you got in that sack?"

The seaman heaved a sigh.

He'll have 'em off me, he thought, that's for sure.

"Rabbits, sir," he said.

"Rabbits?" said the mate.

"Yes, sir," said Jenkins. "Found 'em in among the bales. Don't know how they come to be there."

The mate opened the mouth of the sack and peered in.

"Well, well!" he said. "They'll make a nice meal. Take them down to the galley

and tell the cook I'll have them for my supper."

"Aye, aye, sir," said Jenkins dolefully, but before he could move, the captain of the *Atalanta* appeared, an imposing figure with mutton-chop whiskers, a gold-peaked cap upon his head, and a brass telescope under his arm.

"What's all this, Mister Mate?" he said. "What has that man got in that sack?"

The first mate heaved a sigh. He'll have 'em off me, he thought, that's certain.

"Rabbits, sir," he said.

"Rabbits?" said the captain.

"Yes, sir," said the mate. "Open the sack, Jenkins."

"Well, well," said the captain. "I'm very partial to a nice young rabbit, or better still, two nice young rabbits, under a good, light, pastry crust, with some strips of fat bacon."

He put a hand into the sack and felt the limp forms within.

"Found 'em down below, did you, Jenkins?" he said.

"Yes, sir."

"Heaven only knows how they got there," said the captain, "but one thing's sure. They'll have had no food or water since we sailed. They're as weak as kittens. We must put some flesh on them first. Jenkins, take them to my cabin steward and tell him to see to their needs."

"Aye, aye, sir," said the seaman.

"And Mister Mate," said the captain, "I'd be obliged if you'd have a word with the ship's carpenter. Tell him to knock me up a cage for my rabbits, and to bring it up to my cabin when it's done."

"Aye, aye, sir," said the mate.

"One thing's sure," said the captain. "Once my rabbits have grown a bit and fattened up, they'll be well worth waiting for. I shall enjoy them, Mister Mate. They'll make a nice meal."

CHAPTER SIX

By great good fortune, the captain's cabin steward was a rabbit fancier. Ashore, he kept a shed full of tame ones, and under his expert care Jackson and Bunny soon recovered their health and strength.

Amongst the stores of food that the *Atalunta* had loaded for her voyage was a plentiful supply of vegetables, still fresh, and the two young rabbits gorged happily on cabbage-leaves and carrot-tops and turnip-greens.

In addition, the steward fed them

broken bits of ship's biscuit, and generally looked after them very well. In due course, he knew, the captain would eat them, but that was what rabbits were for.

"Tuck in, my dears," he said, stroking their brown backs. "Enjoy life while you can."

And indeed they did.

"It's funny, you know," said Jackson to Bunny. "Mama told me that men eat rabbits, but that doesn't seem to be true."

"They're certainly treating us well,"

said Bunny with her mouth full. "Both the little one who feeds us and the big one with the whiskers who stands and stares at us. I'm really quite enjoying this voyage now."

"Me too," said Jackson. "I wonder where we shall end up?"

In the captain's pie-dish was of course the answer to this question, and some weeks later the cabin steward's expert advice was sought.

"You keep rabbits at home, Tompkins, don't ye?" said the captain.

"Yes, sir."

"What d'ye think of these two now? Fit to eat, would you say?"

"Well, sir," said the steward, "they're not yet fully grown. I don't reckon they were more than two month old when they come aboard. And we've been at sea eight weeks – that makes 'em four months old now."

"Another four weeks' sailing," said the captain, "and we'll reach Australia. I want to make a meal of them before then."

"Was you going to eat the both of them yourself, sir?" asked the steward.

I was, thought the captain, when they were littler, but now . . . maybe I should give a little dinner, for Sir Hereward and his lady, with rabbit-pie as the main course.

Sir Hereward Potts was a rich and important merchant in the city of London, sailing to Australia with the

intention of becoming the richest and most important merchant in the city of Sydney. He was much the most notable of the *Atalanta's* passengers. A favourable report to the Peninsular and Oriental Navigation Company from Sir Hereward Potts would do the captain no harm at all, and the rabbit-pie would do Sir Hereward a power of good.

"Eat both of them myself, Tompkins?" said the captain in reply to the steward's question. "Of course not. I shall invite Sir Hereward and Lady Potts to share such a treat."

CHAPTER SEVEN

That evening the captain of the *Atalanta* asked the merchant and his wife to his cabin for a glass of wine, and proposed the little dinner party.

"Tomorrow, at about this hour?" he said. That should give Tompkins ample time to see to the preparation of the pie, he thought.

"Delighted, Captain," said Sir Hereward.

"Too kind," said Lady Potts.

Then she caught sight of Jackson and Bunny, lolloping happily about in their cage.

"Oh!" she cried. "How I do love rabbits!"

"So do I," said the captain.

"They are to be the main attraction of our little dinner tomorrow. They are still young and should be very tender, I have no doubt."

Much to the captain's surprise, Lady Potts gave a little scream of horror.

"Oh, Captain!" she cried. "Oh, you could not! Surely you do not mean to kill those charming little creatures? Oh, I could not bear to think of such a thing, much less eat them. Oh, Hereward, must they be slain?"

"My wife is tender-hearted, Captain," said Sir Hereward, and he did not look best pleased.

The captain thought fast.

"I do apologize for suggesting such a thing, your Ladyship," he said. "I had not realized . . . so thoughtless of me."

Stupid woman, he thought, now I shan't be able to eat them, she'll be for ever asking me how they are. There's only one thing to do.

"Sir Hereward," he said with a little bow, "I wonder – would you permit me to present these animals to Lady Potts as a gift, in token of my esteem?"

Sir Hereward looked doubtful.

"The rabbit is unknown in Australia," went on the captain, "and the possession of these two specimens would be in keeping with your wife's position as a leader in colonial society."

Lady Potts gave another little scream, this time of delight, and cried, "Yes! Oh, Captain, yes, how kind of you. Pray have them removed to our quarters for the remainder of the voyage. We shall be delighted to have them, shall we not, Hereward?"

And though Sir Hereward Potts' word was law to thousands in the world of business, he knew better than to cross swords with his wife.

"Yes, my dear," he said. "Delighted."

Thus it was that for the remaining four weeks of the voyage of the *Atalanta* to the Antipodes, the stowaways found themselves in the lap of luxury. Jackson and Bunny were petted and fondled and fed upon the choicest of titbits, and allowed the freedom of the Potts' state-room for much of the day, while, with dustpan and brush, a steward cleaned up behind them.

When at last, at the end of her three-month voyage, the clipper *Atalanta* entered Sydney Harbour, the rabbits were in beautiful condition: fat, sleek and strong.

Sir Hereward had taken a house in the country, some way outside Sydney, and to this he travelled by coach with his wife and all their many pieces of baggage. Among these was the rabbit cage, covered with a sheet to conceal the inmates from prying eyes, for Lady

Potts intended to surprise the colonials with her unusual pets.

When they arrived she insisted that the rabbit cage be unloaded first and placed upon the lawn.

"I must let my little friends stretch their legs," she said to her husband, and she removed the sheet and opened the door of the cage.

Jackson and Bunny hopped out and looked about them.

"We seem to have arrived," said Jackson.

"But where?" said Bunny.

"I have no idea."

"Will they not run away, my dear?" said Sir Hereward.

"Run away?" said Lady Potts. "What an idea! They are much too tame and

much too fond of me, are you not, my dears?" And she bent to stroke them.

"Bunny," said Jackson. "Are you thinking what I'm thinking?"

"Yes," said Bunny. "Let's go!" And side by side they raced away, the first rabbits ever to set foot upon Australian soil.

CHAPTER EIGHT

After all those months cooped up in the *Atalanta* it was sheer bliss to be out in the fresh air again, out in the sunshine (and very hot sunshine it was), and to be free once more.

Jackson and Bunny ran and ran, just for the joy of running, and leaped and twirled and buckjumped (or in Bunny's

case doejumped) in the highest spirits, delighted with one another.

When at last they stopped and looked about them, it was to see a countryside very different from their cool damp homeland. The grass was more brown than green, and the blue-gums looked nothing like English trees. The birds that they saw were strange too – screeching cockatoos and laughing kookaburras and flocks of parrakeets and budgerigars.

Then suddenly Jackson saw a large shape in the distance.

"Quick! Hide!" he said to Bunny, and they scurried for the shelter of some tussocky grass.

"What's the matter?" said Bunny. "You're trembling."

"My dream!" said Jackson. "Do you remember, when we first met in your burrow, I'd been having a bad dream?"

"Yes, I remember."

"Well," said Jackson, "here it comes!" And peering through the grass stems, Bunny saw the most extraordinary animal.

It was as tall as a man, with reddish fur, ears like a donkey, and a face like a sheep. Its arms were short, and it stood upright, balanced upon two enormously strong legs and a long thick tail. Then this monstrous creature began to come towards them, not walking, not running, but hopping in huge bounds on those great hind legs. And as it drew near, Bunny could see something even more

frightening. On the animal's stomach
was a sort of pocket, and out of this
pocket poked another
head, with ears like
a baby donkey
and a face like
a lamb!

"Don't move," whispered Jackson. "It may not see us." And the two rabbits froze, crouching low with ears laid flat back and eyes bulging with terror.

With one last hop the great red kangaroo landed right beside their hiding-place and looked down at them out of her mild sheep's eyes. From her pouch her joey looked down too.

"Ma," he said. "What kind of animals are those?"

"No idea, son," said the mother kangaroo. "Never seen such strange-looking creatures in my whole life. Hold tight now." And away she bounded.

"Fancy calling *us* strange!" said Bunny. "I never set eyes on such weird things as those before."

CHAPTER NINE

As time passed, Jackson and Bunny were to see a great many other odd-looking beasts. As well as kangaroos, they met wallabies and bandicoots and opossums and koalas and numbats and wombats and many more.

There were familiar creatures as well, like cattle and a great many sheep, but one sort of animal they never met.

"It's funny, isn't it?" said Jackson one day. "In this place where we've landed up, wherever it is, there are no other rabbits."

"No," said Bunny, "but there soon will be."

"I don't understand," said Jackson.

But a little later he did, for Bunny scratched herself a nest-burrow and there gave birth to five babies.

"Aren't they lovely!" said Jackson, and indeed, he must have liked babies, because by the end of the rabbits' first year in their new country, Bunny had produced four more litters, totalling twenty-two young in all, and by then she and Jackson were already great-grandparents!

After another year there were hundreds of rabbits in Australia, and then thousands, and then tens of thousands.

Jackson and Bunny lived happily (though not "ever after", because a rabbit's lifespan is not a long one), and by the time they died, peacefully, of old age, there were hundreds of rabbits. And before long

there were millions, and then countless millions, that colonized large stretches of the best land in Australia; a great multitude of rabbits that dug holes everywhere and damaged trees and crops, and ate all the grass meant for the sheep, and drove the Australian settlers to distraction. One of the great plagues in the history of the world it was. And all because of Jackson.

THE END